ADITI

ADVENTURES

THE THAMES DRAGON

SUNITI NAMJOSHI

Pictures
SHEFALEE JAIN

Tulika

What the reviews say...

Suniti Namjoshi, a noted poet, fabulist and writer of feminist and gender issues is also an inspired writer of children's fiction. A brilliant mixture of fable, myth and the modern world, the series introduces us to a repertoire of stories and legends from around the world.... [She] has a simple but lucid prose, effortless to grasp and enjoy.... However, a discerning young reader may intuit the multi-layered sub-texts, twists and plots in the tale.

The Book Review

Aditi and the One-Eyed Monkey, Suniti Namjoshi's first venture into the world of children's fiction, has all the ingredients that fascinate the young.... Written in a simple and entertaining style, the book nevertheless has several layers of meaning. Issues like racism and prejudice have been touched upon.

The New Indian Express

Suniti Namjoshi blends fantasy and current events seamlessly. [*Aditi and the Thames Dragon*] is a good way to introduce children to problems like pollution. There are no immediate cures or magic solutions. It ends on a hopeful note ... A good read."

The Hindu

Though clearly Indian, Namjoshi's characters are reflective of a global sensibility that is at home in different places and in seemingly disparate skins, much like their creator and the current generation of readers.

The Hindu

When a little girl named Aditi embarks on adventures across the world, to help strangers in complicated situations, it is exciting.... But when the author is a feminist, this part adventure, part fantasy tale is more than just a book: It's a bold trend in children's literature.

Women's Feature Service

Suniti updates the traditional mode by including elements that are sure to appeal to a tech-savvy generation.... The trajectory of Aditi's travels, starting out from India and going to many corners of the world, appeals to an urban, English-reading child of today.... But underlying all this the stories of Aditi are still gentle tales dealing with emotions, relationships and courage. They speak of issues such as gender stereotypes, environmental pollution or racism without sounding moralistic.

The Hindu

Namjoshi has built up engaging portraits for her people and animals, foibles and all. Her finest move is to refrain from offering a tempting, permanent solution to these insecurities. Instead, she plays them repeatedly as a riff, showing in every book that while insecurities must exist, it is the best sort of person, or ant or elephant or dragon, who can act for the best in spite of them. In the longer run, this is Namjoshi at her most effortlessly instructive, providing the deepest sort of learning and understanding …

The Book Review

THE FOUR ADVENTURERS

Aditi is a brave little girl, who hates fighting but can wield the Sword of Courage when necessary.

The One-eyed Monkey or **Monkeyji** is older than the others, and so tries hard to be wise and sensible.

The **Ant** loves maps, and wants to measure the world. He sometimes wishes he wasn't quite so small.

The **Elephant** is immensely strong and warm-hearted, and would charge in to help a friend without a thought. She would like to be as logical as the Ant.

OTHER CHARACTERS

The **Sea Dragon** became friends with Aditi and her friends after their first adventure. He now lives with the Island Sage.

The **River Dragon**, a beautiful and gentle creature, is slowly dying in the River Thames because the waters are being poisoned by things thrown into it.

Roshan and **Rohit** are twins who live in London. They ask the adventurers for help to save the River Dragon.

The **Island Sage** lives on an island off the west coast of India and is surrounded by lionesses and their cubs.

Aditi's grandparents are the rulers of a small kingdom in western India. They give Aditi and her friends the Sword of Courage, a cloak of invisibility and some magic clay in order to help them protect themselves.

1

The Letter

Ever since the One-eyed Monkey, the Ant and the Elephant and Aditi herself had dealt with the Dragon who had been scourging her grandparents' kingdom, they had been kept busy solving problems. People who were in trouble often asked them for help, and whenever they could, they did try to help, so that they were liked by almost everyone. Even the Dragon, who had once been their enemy, had over time become their friend.

So far it had been a quiet summer and they were not expecting any trouble. They were sitting on the grass thinking of something pleasant to do. Aditi and the One-eyed Monkey were leaning comfortably against the Elephant's side. The One-eyed Monkey had closed her one grey eye and was fast asleep. The Ant was crawling across an open atlas. He loved travelling and was thinking about where they might go next. Aditi was trying to remember her geography lessons in order to answer the Ant's questions. And as for the Elephant, she looked so peaceful in the morning sunlight that she might have been a statue carved out of grey marble; but she wasn't. She was a flesh and blood elephant, who was feeling a little hungry.

"Let's all go on a picnic," she suddenly suggested.

Aditi laughed because she knew that the Elephant wanted to go into a field and root about for peanuts. She said, "Oh no. Why don't we do something more exciting instead."

The Ant agreed. He said that they had not really seen much of the world and so why didn't they go on a long journey across the ocean and see what there was to see in France or England. The Elephant protested. She hated travelling. She didn't know whether she could get any peanuts or sugarcane in France or England, and anyway she thought that home was best. The Ant and the Elephant had begun a furious argument when the postal parrot landed beside them with the morning post. Most of the letters were for Aditi's grandparents, but there was one letter with a British stamp which was clearly addressed to 'Aditi & Friends'. They wondered who it was from. Aditi opened the letter and read it aloud. It said:

Dear Aditi and Friends,

We would very much like you to visit us, please,
in London. We are in trouble and need your
help. Can you come? The parrot will wait for
your reply and bring it back by return post.

With best wishes,

Roshan and Rohit

P.S. We think our trouble has to do with a River
Dragon. Please let us know if you can help us.

"There!" cried the Ant triumphantly. "Now we'll have
to go to London."

"Where is London?" asked the Elephant. "Is it very far?"

"Yes," replied the One-eyed Monkey, "but they need
our help, so how can we refuse them?"

And Aditi agreed, "Yes, it is far, but we will have to
go. Perhaps we can ask the Dragon to help us." Just as she
said this they saw the Dragon flying overhead. Aditi and
the One-eyed Monkey waved. The Dragon saw them and
began to descend.

The One-eyed Monkey thought that it wasn't really
fair to make the Dragon carry them all and suggested
that they go by aeroplane.

"Well," said Aditi, "I don't know whether an
aeroplane would be big enough. Besides, it would be
expensive..."

They began a long discussion about whether any
aeroplane was big enough to carry the Elephant and if so

which one. The Ant thought that a Jumbo Jet might be big enough or perhaps a Concorde. But when the Dragon joined them and heard that they had been invited to London, he said, "I want to go too and as you see I've grown so big that I could easily carry a Jumbo Jet in each of my claws. It would be no trouble at all for me to carry all of you and fly to England. The Ant and I can soon estimate how long it would take. Oh, do let me go with you. Please? Oh, please?"

And of course, everybody said that yes, the Dragon could go with them.

Aditi then wrote a reply to Roshan and Rohit which she handed over to the parrot. It said:

> Dear Rohit and Roshan,
>
> Thank you for your letter and for your kind invitation. Yes, we will come to London and try to help you. We are leaving tomorrow morning and according to the ant's calculation should arrive there at about midnight (GMT) the day after tomorrow, since on our way to you we shall be flying with the sun. The postal parrot advises us that Shadwell Park would be the best place to land. We look forward to seeing you soon.
>
> With best wishes,
>
> Aditi and Friends

And so the four adventurers and the Dragon began to plan their trip. They agreed that they would take the

Sword of Courage, the cloak of invisibility and the magic clay. These were the weapons that Aditi's grandparents had given them on their first adventure, and very useful they had proved indeed; but the Elephant was thinking of something even more essential. "What about food?" she asked.

The others reassured her on that score. "It's not food that's a problem," the One-eyed Monkey told the Elephant. "It's the River Dragon."

"What is a River Dragon?" asked the Elephant.

But none of them knew. They would have to go to London to help Roshan and Rohit in order to find out.

2

Roshan and Rohit

Roshan and Rohit were sitting in their classroom trying to concentrate on their maths, but it was hard to do so. It was two days now since they had sent their letter. Normally, both Roshan and Rohit paid attention in class. They were twins. Roshan was older than Rohit by a full five minutes and this made her feel she ought to be more responsible, but today they were both scolded by their teacher more than once.

They kept looking out of the window and hoping the parrot would return, but all they could see was the empty patch of grass on which they played during recess. And then suddenly, Roshan saw the parrot. It was tapping on the window pane. She gave Rohit such a dig with her elbow that he exclaimed loudly and got scolded yet again; but he hardly noticed. They could see that the parrot was carrying a letter. Now normally the children would not have played such a trick, but the matter was urgent and so when the teacher wasn't looking Roshan crept away and rang the bell. Everybody thought it was recess time and went into the playground. Roshan and Rohit ran up to the parrot. "Thank you," they cried, "for being so quick!" They read the letter eagerly.

"They say that they'll be arriving at midnight today!" cried Roshan.

"How are they coming?" Rohit wondered.

"The Dragon is flying them over," the parrot replied.

"I hope the Dragon doesn't scare people," Roshan said. Both the children looked worriedly at the parrot.

"It will be all right," the parrot reassured them. "I've told them exactly where to land in Shadwell Park, and as they're arriving at midnight, with any luck no one will notice them."

$$14 \times 7 = 98$$
$$14 \times 8 = 112$$
$$14 \times 9 = 126$$
$$14 \times 10 = 140$$

"Oh, thank you!" cried the children.

"That's all right" said the parrot. "And now I'm very tired and I'm going to bed."

The parrot flew away and very soon afterwards the bell rang. Rohit and Roshan had to go back into the classroom. Their teacher was sitting there looking puzzled. She had never known the morning session to pass so quickly or the recess to seem so long. All that afternoon poor Roshan and Rohit tried to work, but they kept thinking about Aditi and her friends and whether they would arrive in time to be able to help.

At last school was over and as they walked home Roshan and Rohit looked fearfully at the Thames. The water level was higher than ever and in some places the river had overflowed its banks. Most of the rubbish and junk in the river was covered up by the water. Even as they watched the water seemed to rise higher and higher. There was serious danger of a flood, but everyone thought that the danger would disappear as soon as it stopped raining so much. Roshan and Rohit knew better. They had actually seen the River Dragon. The trouble was that nobody believed them. When they had tried to tell everyone that the true reason for the flooding of the Thames was that the River Dragon had woken up, people had just said, "Oh, don't be silly! Don't you know that dragons are just a lot of mythical nonsense." That was when they had sent their urgent message to Aditi and her friends.

That night Roshan and Rohit made their plans carefully. When it was their bedtime they went to bed without any fuss and pretended to go to sleep. Then, as soon as they were sure that their parents had fallen asleep, they quickly put on their clothes and their boots, and

having equipped themselves with two umbrellas and a powerful torch, they crept out of the house through the kitchen window.

They walked towards the park in the darkness. They were a little afraid because it was so late at night and also because of the cars speeding by. The bit where they had to walk through a tunnel in order to come up by the gates of the park was the worst, but they did it. And when they found that the park gates were locked, they climbed over them. Then they walked to the open space in the park and waited. At least it had stopped raining. They wondered how long they would have to wait, but it wasn't long at all. As they looked up at the sky they saw a great black shadow blotting out the clouds. For a moment they did not know what it was. Then they realised it was the Dragon. They waved their hands and Rohit flashed the torch.

There was a great rush of air and the Dragon landed. The trees shuddered in the wind and one or two of them were blown down. (The next day the weather people spoke of a small hurricane.) Rohit and Roshan ran forward to greet Aditi and her friends. Everybody said hello to each other and then Roshan explained the urgency of the problem and Rohit added, "With your Dragon we are sure you will be able to overcome our River Dragon."

"Hold on!" cried the Dragon. "Dragons are not allowed to fight each other, and besides, I'm not sure I would win if I fought a River Dragon. And anyway, I don't want to."

"But people fight each other," Rohit remarked. He was taken aback by the Dragon's response.

The Dragon just looked stubborn. "That may be as it may be. Perhaps in that particular respect dragons have more sense than people. Look, I'm much too big to remain here. I shall go away now, but I'll be back soon."

"Where are you going?" asked the One-eyed Monkey.

"To see the Sage," the Dragon replied. "The secret weapons you have are no use to me. The Sword of Courage is much too small, besides I have my talons. I could not manipulate the magic clay with which the little Ant can make anything at all. But even if I could, I don't think I could concentrate for more than two seconds to keep it in existence. I've seen the Ant concentrate for minutes at a time! As for the cloak of invisibility, if I tried to put it on, it would barely cover one of my ears! No, the Sage has always been kind to me. I'm going to ask her please to give me something special that I can use."

With that the Dragon flew away. The sage lived on a small island off the west coast of India. Would the Dragon return?

Everybody was most disappointed. How were they going to deal with the River Dragon without another dragon to help them? They also had another problem: where were they going to put the Elephant?

3

A Night of Preparations

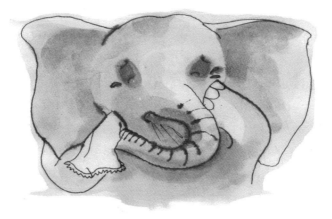

Rohit watched the Dragon fly away and wondered why a creature that size needed a secret weapon, and what it was exactly that the Dragon had in mind. His attention was recalled to what was happening around him by the Elephant's sneezing. A steady drizzle had begun. Aditi flung the cloak of invisibility around the Elephant. This had the effect of making the Elephant disappear. Roshan and Rohit watched fascinated.

"Will the cloak keep her dry?" inquired Roshan.

"No," replied the invisible Elephant so mournfully

that Roshan and Rohit realised that they had better hurry up and lead their visitors to some shelter.

They took their friends to an old shed behind the football field, and though the Elephant had trouble squeezing in, she managed somehow. Once they were all safely inside, they set about making it comfortable. The Ant used his magic clay to provide them with brooms with which they quickly swept out the shed, and then he made them a hammer and a saw and various other tools with which they converted empty packing cases into useful furniture. Every now and then the Ant's concentration would falter and the others would find themselves grasping empty air instead of a tool, but on the whole the Ant concentrated remarkably well and they were soon done.

Roshan and Rohit apologised to the adventurers for not having been able to find better quarters for them, but the One-eyed Monkey just smiled and said that they were comfortable, thank you. And indeed, as Rohit and Roshan looked about them, it was so reassuring to be with friends that the little shed did look cosy and comfortable. Both Rohit and Roshan were aware that the adventurers had flown a long way and must be tired. They were torn between wanting to tell the visitors about the impending danger and their desire to let the adventurers rest.

Aditi seemed to guess what was going on in their minds. "Tell us about the danger," she said gently.

Roshan hesitated. "You must be very tired..."

Aditi smiled. "No, it's all right. We managed to sleep on the Dragon's back. Tell us about it."

And so Roshan and Rohit told Aditi and her friends about the River Dragon. "You see," Rohit concluded, "something is making the River Dragon angrier and angrier and when she lashes her tail the river overflows. What we are really afraid of is that one of these days the River Dragon will wake up properly and then the river

will really boil over and destroy all our houses and our school and drown this area in river water."

"We tried to tell people about the River Dragon," Roshan added, "but they wouldn't believe us. They said it was just the junk moving about in the muddy river and that dragons are mythical. That's why we wrote to you. We thought you would know about River Dragons."

This made Aditi, the Elephant, the One-eyed Monkey and the Ant feel a little embarrassed. At last Aditi said, "We would like to help you, but the truth is that none of us knows anything at all about River Dragons."

The Elephant, seeing the children look disappointed, added quickly, "But I'm sure we can find out."

"Yes, I'm sure we can," Aditi said thoughtfully. "Someone somewhere must know about them. Perhaps it's in a book."

"I know," cried Roshan suddenly. "I'm sure there must be a book in the British Museum in which it's all written down."

"What is the British Museum?" inquired the Elephant.

"It's where all the ancient maps are kept," the Ant informed her.

"And ancient manuscripts," added Aditi.

"And ancient carvings and sculptures," put in the One-eyed Monkey.

"Is everything in it ancient?" asked the Elephant.

"Pretty much," Rohit replied.

"Well, we can walk there tomorrow. It should be interesting," said the Elephant happily. It was obvious that she was looking forward to going to the British Museum.

Now it was Roshan and Rohit who felt awkward. "It's too far to walk," ventured Rohit.

"Nonsense," said the Elephant. "We have often walked miles and miles, haven't we, Aditi?"

"Yes, I know," said Roshan, "but to walk there would take time, and the water is rising minute by minute. Besides, there's the traffic. That would be a problem."

"What is 'traffic'," asked the Elephant, "and why would it be a problem?"

"Traffic consists of people and motor cars. They would stare at you and honk at you because you would hold it up."

"I would hold it up?" The Elephant was puzzled. "And why would they stare at me? Aren't they used to Elephants?"

"No," Rohit said. "Elephants are unusual."

The Elephant smiled at him uncertainly. "I suppose that's good?"

It was Rohit's turn to look uncertain. "Well, I don't know... But you see you would hold up the traffic, because you would be much too slow."

"Oh." The Elephant was feeling most disappointed. She wanted very much to go with the others. "Couldn't I wear the cloak of invisibility?"

"But then everyone would bump into you," Roshan said. She felt sorry for the Elephant, but she wasn't sure that the Elephant would be able to cope with London traffic.

"Well, how were you going to go?" persisted the Elephant.

"By bus."

"Well, that's all right then. I'll go by bus too."

"You wouldn't fit into a bus."

"Oh. I haven't flown all this way just to sit in a shed. I want to have a look at London." The Elephant was beginning to get bad-tempered, and it was obvious that everyone was feeling tired and sleepy.

The One-eyed Monkey intervened. "Let's sleep on it," she suggested, "and see what we can do tomorrow." She looked at Rohit and Roshan. "Is it safe for you to go home at this hour?"

"It's not exactly safe," Rohit replied, "but we'll be all right."

"Nonsense." The Elephant rose to her feet majestically. "I'll take you home. Here, get on my back and put on the cloak of invisibility. No one will see us, but even if they do I doubt very much that even in London anyone would want to tangle with an elephant."

The children accepted gratefully, and the Elephant too felt pleased about being able to do something useful. She hated feeling that she was just in the way and a nuisance to the others. They made their way through the deserted streets. Occasionally a car roared past. Roshan and Rohit felt a lot safer on their way home than they had felt coming out to the park. They paused by the river and stared at the black water, but the River Dragon was not showing herself tonight. The Elephant took the children home and returned to the shed, where she went to sleep with the others, but her dreams were troubled. All night long she dreamt that a lot of noisy motor cars kept bumping into her.

4

The Bus Trip

A watery sun trickled in through a crack in the door. Aditi rubbed her eyes. Sleeping beside her was a miniature dragon. The tiny creature seemed real enough and was even snoring quietly. Aditi decided that she hadn't woken up properly and was still dreaming. Then the dragon opened one blue eye and spoke to her. "Don't you recognise me? I'm still the same Dragon, only smaller." By this time the others had woken up and Roshan and Rohit had arrived with some breakfast. The Elephant let them in and they all returned to stare at the Dragon.

"How did you become smaller?" asked the Elephant.

The Dragon smiled at them. "The Sage gave me a secret weapon." He held up a jar of sandalwood ointment. "When you rub it on, you grow smaller. The effect lasts for six hours. I have about five hours left, but then I must

go away again, because I'll start to grow bigger." For a moment Rohit imagined the Dragon growing bigger and bigger in the heart of London. There would be terrible accidents. His wings would knock down buildings. The Dragon himself might get hurt. Rohit glanced down at the miniature Dragon, now curled up on Aditi's shoulder, to reassure himself that none of this had actually happened. He admired the Dragon. The slightest movement made the light ripple along the Dragon's scales as though he was made of living metal.

Over breakfast they discussed their plans. "It would be best to go to the British Museum by bus," Roshan explained. "That way we'll be able to show you more of London."

"Yes and now I can go too!" the Elephant said happily. The others smiled at her. They knew she had realised how the Dragon's ointment could be put to good use.

The Elephant turned to Roshan, "Last night I carried you. Today will you carry me?"

"Gladly!" Roshan replied. She felt so honoured to have been asked to carry the Elephant.

"And will you carry me?" the Dragon asked Rohit.

"Delighted," Rohit answered, beaming with pleasure.

Breakfast was soon done, and after they had rubbed some of the ointment on the Elephant and made her smaller, they all set off. The Dragon snuggled under Rohit's shirt, the Elephant settled down in Roshan's pocket and peered out over the top, while the Ant perched on the One-eyed Monkey and she in turn perched on Aditi's shoulder. They walked through the park to the bus stop. "It's all very green, isn't it? Is it all like this?" asked the Elephant. "It would be very pleasant if it didn't rain so much."

"But if it didn't rain so much," Roshan replied, "it wouldn't be so green. Doesn't it rain in India?"

"Only during the rainy season," the Elephant replied, as though that's how things should be in a well-ordered world.

"What about the rest of the time?"

"In the summer the sun shines and it's hot, and in the winter the sun shines and it's not so hot."

Roshan considered. "I suppose there wouldn't be any need for weather forecasts," she thought to herself. She wasn't sure she herself would like such predictable weather.

When they came to the river they all stopped and

stared at the water. "Oh, I think I see her! I see her!" the Ant cried out in sudden excitement.

"Where? Oh where?"

"There. There's something brown moving near that sunken boat."

But the water was so dirty and there was so much rubbish in the river, that it was hard to see. "Let's come back later when we know more about River Dragons," said the One-eyed Monkey. She was afraid that their time would run out and that the Elephant and the Dragon would start growing bigger and bigger.

They made their way to the bus stop and waited. Soon a red double-decker bus came along. The Elephant was enchanted. "That bus is bigger than me," she confided to Roshan. "I might have fitted inside, after all."

"But it's meant to carry lots of passengers," Roshan told her.

Once they were inside the bus, the Elephant looked around. "Yes," she said, "I see what you mean."

They climbed to the top of the bus and took seats right at the front. "Now," Rohit said to the visitors, "from here you'll get a good view of London. It will take us about an hour to get to the museum."

"Is it very far?" inquired the Ant.

"Well, no."

"Then why will it take us so long?"

Rohit pointed to the traffic below them. "Because the traffic is so slow."

"Why is it slow?"

"Too many cars."

"Why do people use motor cars?" It was the Elephant this time. Rohit didn't know what to say. "Because they think it would be faster."

"But you just said —"

Before the bus journey was over the Elephant had managed to ask a dozen other questions. Why does it rain so much? Where are the animals? Why are there so many motor cars? Why aren't there any elephants? Well, cows at least? Where is the sun? Are England and London the same? Roshan and Rohit had done their best to provide answers. Meanwhile the bus had crawled on its way past clothes shops and newsagents, TV shops and telephone booths, hamburger joints and cinema theatres, old buildings and new ones, and had at last brought them to the museum.

They walked through the iron gates and entered the museum without any difficulty. They found the section where the old books were displayed. Though many of the books had been shifted to the new Reading Room, they even found the book that was the authoritative text on the nature of dragons, and then they faced a problem. The book was locked inside a glass-topped cabinet, and though the book was open, it was open at the wrong page. The one-eyed monkey could read the writing without difficulty, but it described the habits of Red Dragons.

The One-eyed Monkey groaned. Where one of the pages had swung up a little, she could see that the following page was about River Dragons. "Oh, if I could only turn that page somehow!" she cried in frustration. The others stared at the illustration of a Red Dragon.

"Perhaps we could apply for permission to look at this book?" Aditi ventured.

Roshan and Rohit both shook their heads. "It would take too long," Roshan explained. "The River Dragon could begin lashing her tail any moment now. Any delay could be dangerous. We tried looking up River Dragons on the internet, but there wasn't enough information. And we tried emailing you, but the email bounced. And now there's almost no time left."

"I could climb into the cabinet through a crack," offered the Ant, and before anyone could stop him, he ran along the side of the cabinet and slipped through. They could see him clearly now through the glass top. He climbed up the side of the book and slipped under the page that had swung up. Then he braced himself against the page below and pushed as hard as he could. Nothing happened, but the Ant was very persistent. He kept trying to turn the page over. The others watched anxiously, afraid that he would wear himself out. The Ant even tried leaping upwards in order to push as far as possible against the outside edge of the book. It was no use.

The Ant then climbed on top of the swinging page, which hardly bent under his weight, and looked hard at the Elephant. The Elephant nodded. They couldn't talk to each other because of the glass, but the Elephant knew what to do. She took the magic clay from Aditi and with the help of the miniature Dragon she fashioned a pole that was about two inches long and as thin as a needle. They showed this to the Ant. The Ant waved back and concentrated on the pole. Soon he had a metal pole in his pincers. He reared up and prodded mightily at the very edge of the swinging page. The effort overbalanced him and he fell right off the edge of the book; but the page swung up. At the very top it teetered for a fraction of a second, and finally turned over. The book was now open at River Dragons. The Ant looked anxiously at the Elephant. She nodded vigorously. Through the glass they could see that he was cheering. He climbed up the side of the cabinet and out through a crack. He had bruised

himself a little. Everyone made a fuss about him, but he just thanked the Dragon and the Elephant for giving him the magic pole. Then they settled down to study the River Dragon staring at them out of the book.

5

What the Book Said

The River Dragon was no colour and every colour. She was all the colours that water can be. Sometimes they could see her shape in the water, and sometimes it looked as though she had merged with the water and it was hard to say which was which. The artist who had done the picture had liked River Dragons. The One-eyed Monkey began to read the text aloud. Rohit and Roshan wrote it down.

"Habitat: Rivers," said the One-eyed Monkey.

"What does that mean?" asked the Elephant.

"It means," Aditi told her, "that River Dragons live in rivers."

"But we already knew that." The Elephant was indignant.

Rohit smiled at her. "Sometimes books tell you things you already know."

"What else does it say?"

The One-eyed Monkey peered at the book. She read slowly. "Characteristics: They breathe out foaming white water. They have wings like fins and a long tail.

They like fish. They do not eat them. They are vegetarians. On the whole they prefer moderate temperatures... Size: Among dragons, average."

"Well then, she'll be about my size. Perhaps we'll become friends." The little Dragon sounded happy.

"Well, I don't know," the One-eyed Monkey frowned. "It says here that River Dragons are delicate and sensitive."

"What does that mean exactly?" asked the Elephant.

"It means that they get sick easily and they get hurt easily," Roshan told her.

"Does it say anything at all about how to talk to them?" Roshan asked.

The One-eyed Monkey scrutinised the book. "It says here that they are shy and unsociable, but make excellent friends once you get to know them. The problem seems to be in getting to know them."

"We could try speaking to the River Dragon politely," Aditi suggested.

"That won't be enough," the One-eyed Monkey replied. "It says here that they won't answer unless you call them by a name that really pleases them."

"But how can we know what name the River Dragon would find pleasing unless she talks to us first and tells us?" asked the Elephant petulantly.

The One-eyed Monkey shrugged. "Well, that's the difficulty. We'll just have to guess and keep trying until we hit on something she likes."

"Does the book offer any advice?" Rohit asked.

"No, that's all it says," the One-eyed Monkey answered.
"We had better go now and see what we can do."

All the way back on the bus they tried to think of
names that the River Dragon might possibly like to be
called. At one point Roshan and the Elephant got into a
heated discussion. The Elephant was convinced that
Peanuts was the only possible name for a River Dragon,
and when Roshan wouldn't agree she got very cross. Some
of the other passengers in the bus began staring at them.
Roshan noticed this and to prevent any further
complications said loudly to Aditi, "Don't you like my
toy elephant?" And Aditi replied, "Oh yes, she's very
sweet." All this annoyed the Elephant so much that she
kept quiet for the next half hour and by that time it was
time to get off the bus.

They walked down to the river to the spot where
Roshan and Rohit had seen the River Dragon. They had

thought of a great many names and they began trying them all.

"O Lotus of the Nile," Aditi called.

"Isn't that a bit farfetched?" asked the little Dragon. It obviously was since nothing happened.

"O Breather of White Foam from Whose Nostrils Jets of Water Shoot with a Force Greater than any Elephant's." The Elephant managed to say all this without pausing for breath. They all stared at her in astonishment.

"Is that a name?" asked Rohit, genuinely puzzled.

"It could be," replied the Elephant.

"But I thought you were convinced that the River Dragon's name was really Peanuts," Roshan protested.

"Well, and so it probably is, but that might not be the name by which she might like to be called. Besides, I thought she would like it if I said she was stronger than an elephant." By this time the Elephant's logic had got so complicated that nobody dared to protest. In any event it looked as if the River Dragon was unimpressed. They stared at the water, and though they thought they could detect small movements in the muddy browns and greens, the River Dragon did not answer.

They tried many different names: Jewel, Rose, Dazzler, Star, Beauty, Beast, Bashful... They got carried away and started again: Sea-Rose, Sea-Queen, Sea-Star, Water-Dragon, Water-Beast, Water-Beauty and so forth. Nothing worked. Rohit called out, "Daisy, Daffodil, Buttercup!"

They all stared at him. "What are you doing?" the One-eyed Monkey asked.

Rohit explained, "I thought we could try calling her by the names of all the things we liked. I like flowers."

"Yes, all right," the Ant agreed. "Tractor, Bulldozer!" he called out as loudly as he could. But nothing happened.

The Elephant even tried, "Sugarcane and Condensed Milk." It was useless, and as time began to run out and they became more and more desperate, the names became more and more absurd. The little Dragon was almost in tears. He knew that any moment now he would begin to grow bigger and they had still not succeeded in making contact with the River Dragon.

"Friend!" he called out in complete despair. "Oh Friend, won't you answer?"

And with that they saw what they had thought was an island of junk and debris in the middle of the river stir sluggishly. A faint voice reached them: "Who calls me Friend? I have no friends."

The little Dragon could hardly restrain himself. "I am your friend," he called out as strongly as he could. "I too have known what it is to be friendless. I am your friend, as are all the others here if only you would not threaten them."

"I threaten no one," came that tired voice again.

"When you lash your tail, the river overflows. You will drown us," Rohit cried out.

"I was in pain. Soon it will be over."

"But what is the matter?" cried out the Elephant.

"Poison. The river has been poisoned." The voice was becoming weaker and weaker.

"Can you hold on?" Aditi called out. "We'll bring you help."

"Yes." But the River Dragon's reply was faint and barely reached them.

6

The Rescue

The little Dragon was desperate with fear for the River Dragon. Rohit had to hold on to him with both hands in order to prevent him from jumping into the river. "It won't help," Rohit told him. "Stay here and keep up her spirits. I'll run to the shed and fetch the pot of sandalwood ointment so that we can make her smaller and rescue her." He thrust the little Dragon into Aditi's hands and started towards the park.

"And I'll run home and fetch a bowl of fresh water in which we can put her once she's rescued," Roshan called out over her shoulder.

The four adventurers and the little Dragon stared across the water at the River Dragon. "Can you hear us?" Aditi called out.

A faint movement of the tail was the River Dragon's reply.

"She's very weak," Aditi murmured.

"Hold on," the little Dragon called out to her. "We'll have you out of there soon. It won't be long now."

The One-eyed Monkey was frowning. "Exactly how are we going to get the ointment to the River Dragon and get her out of the river before she shrinks and slips out of our hands?" she murmured to Aditi. "She isn't strong enough to swim towards us."

"I'll swim to her," the little Dragon volunteered.

Aditi and the One-eyed Monkey shook their heads. "You are too little," Aditi told him. "The current will carry you away."

This so surprised the Dragon that for a moment he was quiet. It was probably the first time in his life that he had been told that he was too little to do anything.

"I don't think that any of us is strong enough," the One-eyed Monkey went on. "The current is very powerful at this point."

Just then Roshan and Rohit came dashing up. "Is she still all right?" Roshan asked.

"Yes, is she?" the Elephant piped up from Roshan's pocket.

"I think so," Aditi replied, "but how are we to get the ointment to her? If only we had a rope..." Even as she spoke she found she was holding a coil of rope in her hand. The Ant had been busy.

"We are throwing you a rope," the little Dragon called out. "Just hold on to it and we'll drag you ashore."

Aditi threw the rope and they saw the River Dragon move feebly in an effort to catch it, but there was no strength left in her and the end of the rope drifted away.

This was too much for the little Dragon. He seized the pot of ointment between his jaws and dived into the river. The current caught him at once and began to carry him downstream. But then, under their very eyes, an extraordinary thing happened. The little Dragon began to grow. The current was now of no consequence to him. In no time at all, he had reached the River Dragon. He was growing so rapidly that he had almost reached his full size. With a tremendous effort, he half lifted the River Dragon out of the water and dragged her to the shore. The water level sank by nearly a foot. "Quick! Cover her with the cloak of invisibility and put the ointment on her. Then heal her as best you can," the Dragon cried out. He tossed down the ointment to them, and with a stroke of his wings which sent the water in the river running backwards, he soared out of sight.

The others had been knocked almost breathless by the speed with which everything had happened, but they

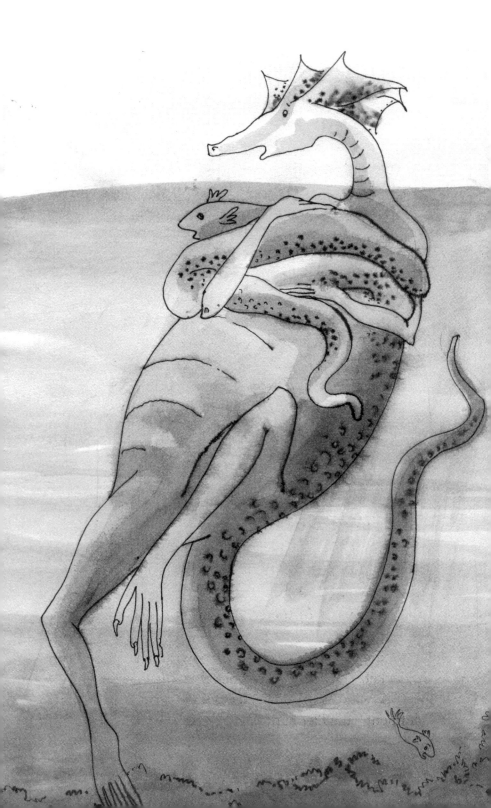

rallied quickly. Aditi and the One-eyed Monkey began anointing the River Dragon while Rohit and Roshan covered her with the cloak as well as they could. They knew from experience that the ointment would require a few minutes to work and they didn't want passers-by to gather around the helpless dragon. When the River Dragon had been reduced in size, Roshan picked her up gently and was about to lower her into the goldfish bowl, when the One-eyed Monkey shouted, "Stop!"

Everyone looked at her in surprise. "Why?" asked Roshan.

"I've been thinking about what happened just now," the One-eyed Monkey replied. "Reduce the water in the bowl so that there is only a little bit of water at the bottom. If she's entirely covered in water, then all the ointment will be washed off and she'll grow back to her normal size. Don't you see, that's what happened to the little Dragon. All the ointment got washed off."

"Yes, you're right." Roshan emptied the bowl of most of its water. Then she made a bed of weeds at the bottom and lowered the little River Dragon onto it gently. They looked at the little River Dragon. Her eyes were closed, but she was still breathing. Her removal from the poisoned water of the river seemed to have done her some good.

Rohit picked up the goldfish bowl and half hid it with his jacket. They all walked back towards the shed.

"As soon as we get back I'm going to wash off all this ointment," the Elephant declared. "I didn't know that all

it took was a little water. If I had known that, the little
Dragon needn't have risked his life. I could have helped."

"But even a full-sized elephant wouldn't have been
strong enough to drag the River Dragon out of the water,"
Aditi told her.

For some reason, this seemed to console the Elephant.
"Oh well," she murmured, "that's all right then."

"I wish there was an ointment that made small
creatures bigger," the Ant said wistfully.

Rohit looked at him. "If you were as big as a dragon
or even only as big as an elephant, you would probably
be the strongest creature on earth," he informed him.

"Would I?" asked the Ant.

"Yes," Roshan replied. "For their size, ants are quite extraordinarily strong."

"Yes," the Elephant added. "Do you remember when you turned the page in the British Museum? It wasn't just the pole, it was also your strength that helped you to do it. I'm not sure that I could have. For me it would have been like turning a piece of the sky or taking the roof off a large flat building. It was hard."

The Ant was getting embarrassed. "When do you suppose the Dragon will return?" he asked.

"I don't know," the One-eyed Monkey replied. "Perhaps tonight or tomorrow. Perhaps he has gone to consult the Sage and find out the proper treatment."

Rohit peered at the River Dragon under his jacket. "She's still asleep," he said.

Roshan and Rohit looked at one another anxiously. They hoped that for the River Dragon help had not come too late. They slipped into the shed and put down the River Dragon.

"We must go home now or our parents will worry," Roshan said. "We'll come back later."

"No, you need a good night's sleep," the One-eyed Monkey told them. "Come back early tomorrow morning. We all need to rest. Aditi will go with you and buy us some food."

"What about the River Dragon?" the children protested.

Aditi smiled at them. "She'll be all right. We'll take turns watching over her all night."

"All right," Roshan agreed. "We'll be here early

tomorrow and then you can rest. It's Sunday tomorrow and after that it's the holidays."

The three children walked away. As they passed the river, they noticed that the water level had sunk considerably. "Well, at least we don't have to worry about the river flooding. Thank you for helping us." Roshan sighed. "I ought to feel happy, but somehow I feel more worried than ever."

They stared at the murky water. "Do you really suppose it's poisonous?" Aditi had spoken her thoughts aloud.

Roshan and Rohit thought of the sick River Dragon. "Yes," Rohit answered sadly. "Yes, it must be."

7

A Turn for the Worse

They divided up the night into two-hour shifts among themselves. The Elephant had the first watch. She was now back to her normal size. By the light of a solitary candle she peered at the sleeping River Dragon. "Besides giving her a little water if she wakes up, what am I supposed to do?" The Elephant was worried. She wanted to do her best, but she didn't really know very much about looking after River Dragons.

"That's all you have to do," Aditi reassured her. "If she takes a turn for the worse, just wake us up."

"But how will I know if she has taken a turn for the worse?" the Elephant asked.

The One-eyed Monkey tried to remember exactly what the book had said. "Do you see these opalescent colours that play along her scales? Should that play of colours ever stop or grow dim in any way, then wake us up."

"All right," said the Elephant and settled down to watch over the River Dragon. "Is there anything else I should know?"

"If she has difficulty breathing or develops a temperature, then let us know," Aditi told her.

"But how will I know if she develops a fever?"

"They change colour," the One-eyed Monkey told her briefly. "Just wake us up if you think anything is wrong."

But the River Dragon slept quietly through the Elephant's watch and through the One-eyed Monkey's watch and even through Aditi's watch. It wasn't until about five o'clock in the morning when the Ant was on duty that something began to go wrong.

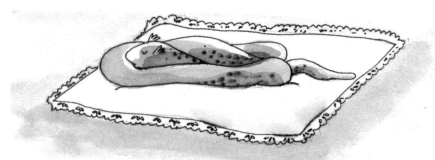

The Ant rubbed his eyes. The opalescent play of colours hadn't faded, but the River Dragon seemed to be turning blue. The change in colour was very slight. Perhaps he was imagining it? Should he wake up the others? He pressed his face against the glass bowl and drew back startled. The glass had felt icy cold. He hurried away to wake up the others. "I don't think the River Dragon is running a fever," he told Aditi. "I think the problem is just the opposite. I think we had better do something quickly to keep her warm."

They took the River Dragon out of the bowl and set her down on a dry handkerchief near the candle. "But is it all right to take her out of the water?" the Elephant asked.

"Yes," the One-eyed Monkey replied, "as long as we give her a drink every now and then."

They then wrapped her up in a silk scarf and watched over her. Though she didn't seem to be getting any colder, she didn't seem to be getting any warmer either. Nor did she once open her eyes.

At about six in the morning the window at the back of the shed burst open and the little Dragon flew in. "Is she all right?" he asked.

"No," Aditi replied. "She's freezing. We don't seem to be able to keep her warm enough."

"The Sage warned me about that," the Dragon replied. "We'll have to build a fire. I saw Roshan and Rohit on their way here. Tell them to gather all the firewood they can."

Roshan and Rohit arrived and began to gather firewood. "The wood is damp," Roshan told the Dragon.

"Never mind," the Dragon replied. "I'll breathe flames onto it until it catches fire."

Soon they had a pile of firewood ready at a safe distance from the shed and the little Dragon blew on it until at last it caught fire.

"Now what do we do?" Rohit asked.

"Now you must place the River Dragon in the centre of the fire," the little Dragon told them.

"But she'll burn," protested the Elephant.

"Dragons don't burn, and nor does the ointment," the little Dragon replied. "It's all right. I've consulted the Sage. Do as I say or she'll freeze to death."

Aditi approached the sleeping River Dragon. The play of colours seemed to have become dimmer and the bluish colour had deepened. Aditi picked her up tenderly. "Are you sure?" asked Aditi.

"Yes!" replied the little Dragon. "Hurry! Put her in the fire."

But Aditi could not bear to put the River Dragon into the fire. She held her over the fire while the flames scorched her hands.

"No, that won't do," the little Dragon shouted. He jumped into the fire himself. The flames licked about him so that it was hard to tell which was the Dragon and which the fire. "Look! Can't you see? Dragons don't burn. Give her to me. I'll hold her."

Aditi handed the River Dragon to the little Dragon in the middle of the fire. The flames grew in their fury and intensity. For a few moments no one could see the two dragons. Then the flames died down and left the two dragons standing in the ashes. The River Dragon blinked at them. Her eyes were like emeralds, her scales shone silver and the play of colours was so quick and so dazzling that it was difficult to look at her.

"Her name is Opal," the little Dragon said. "She'll be all right now."

The others helped them out of the ashes. "Welcome Opal," they all said to her. They took her inside the shed and set her down on the silk scarf.

"Will you really be all right now?" the Elephant asked.

"Yes," replied Opal. "I'll be all right for a little while. Thank you for helping me."

"It was really the little Dragon who helped you most," Aditi told her.

"The little Dragon? Oh you mean Goldie!"

"Goldie?" The others looked at the River Dragon in astonishment. Then they turned on the little Dragon. "You never told us that was your name!" Aditi exclaimed.

"As long as there was only one of me, I didn't need a name," the little Dragon, Goldie, explained. "I was just the Dragon. Opal gave me my name. She said it suited me."

"Goldie," everyone murmured to themselves, trying to get used to it. "It's quite a nice name," the Elephant pronounced judiciously. "Why did you choose it?"

"Because he's golden-hearted," Opal replied.

The little Dragon was so surprised he fell over. The One-eyed Monkey picked him up and set him on his feet. "Yes," she said, "he is a good fellow."

The little Dragon was so pleased and so embarrassed that he just squirmed a little and didn't say anything. But the Ant was frowning. He had been thinking. He turned to Opal. "Why did you say that you would only be all right for a little while?" he asked. "Is it because of the river?"

Opal sighed. "You see," she said, "in some way I'm a part of the river. I can live away from it for days at a time. Perhaps even months though I've never tried it. But sooner or later I must return to the river."

"The river wasn't always the way it is now," she added softly. "There was a time when the water was sparkling and clear."

"But what is it exactly that has poisoned the river?" Goldie asked.

"Things."

"What things?"

"Things that people have thrown into it over the years."

8

The Strange and the Unusual

They had spent the morning discussing ways and means of cleaning up the river, and though the sun was shining and they were sitting outside the shed and had had breakfast, they were beginning to feel disheartened. The Ant had calculated that if they rigged up a system of ropes and pulleys, and then if each of them spent seven hours a day for seventy years pulling rubbish out of the river, it would still not make very much difference. "You see," he had explained, "all the time that we were pulling rubbish out, people would be throwing more rubbish in. And then, of course, there's the problem of chemicals, the poisonous substances that have dissolved in the water and are hard to remove."

"But you can't step into the same river twice," the One-eyed Monkey had protested. "The water in the river flows away. That's why people throw things into it. They want it to carry away their rubbish."

"But then it just poisons the sea," Goldie had growled.

"And besides, the poisoned water kills living things. We've got to stop people from throwing in rubbish."

"How?" Rohit had asked.

"We could explain it all to them," the One-eyed Monkey had suggested. She was a great believer in explaining things.

But Rohit and Roshan had looked doubtful. "People don't listen," Roshan had said. "We tried to tell them about Opal and about the danger of the river flooding, but they didn't believe us. And now they'd just say that we were making a nuisance of ourselves and making up things."

It was at this point when the discussion had ground to a halt that Opal who had been dozing and resting in the sun, suddenly woke up and said, "We'll show them."

Everyone stared at her. "What do you mean?" Goldie asked.

"Well, we'll show them that River Dragons exist, but that if they keep throwing rubbish into the water, they won't exist for much longer," Opal replied.

"Yes!" cried Goldie excitedly. "And Sea Dragons! I must be a Sea Dragon since I was born in a cave beside the sea. And I exist!"

"And Well Dragons," added Opal. "The little dragons who live in wells — they're poisoning them as well."

"And ordinary fish," put in the One-eyed Monkey.

"And whales and dolphins," offered the Elephant.

"And the lobsters and crayfish, and the crabs and cuttlefish," the Ant joined in.

"And all the seaweeds and all the plants in the rivers and the seas." This was from Aditi.

Then they all paused and looked at one another. "What is happening really is terrible," Rohit murmured.

And Roshan added, "We'll have to try to do something about it. We'll have to tell everyone."

"Well, what's the best way of telling everyone?" asked the Ant.

"The press," Rohit replied, "or radio and television."

"Well," said the Ant. "Let's just walk up to them and tell them."

But Roshan and Rohit hesitated. "It's not that simple," Roshan said.

"Why not?" demanded Goldie.

"Well, you see," Roshan tried to explain. "Lots of people would like to put lots of things in the newspapers, and lots of people would like to see themselves on television or hear themselves on radio. They can't put everyone in, so you see they don't just listen to anyone."

"Well then, how do you say what you want to say in the papers or on radio or on television? And which of these is the best?" asked the Elephant.

"Well, you can pay to do it. It's called 'taking an ad'. And perhaps for our purpose, television is the best because it reaches the most people. But it's also the most expensive."

"Should we take an ad?" inquired Aditi.

Roshan shook her head decisively. "No. We couldn't afford it. And besides, no one would believe us."

"Why not?" asked the One-eyed Monkey.

"Because it's an ad."

The One-eyed Monkey shook her head over this. "It seems very strange," she murmured. "Isn't there any other way to get on television?"

"Well, I suppose we could be a news item..." Rohit said hesitantly.

"What is a 'news item'?"

"Anything that has happened that they choose to say has happened."

"But what sort of thing?" persisted the One-eyed Monkey.

"It's hard to be sure," Rohit confessed. "Sometimes it's about war and things like that, but sometimes a war can be going on for months and nothing is said. I — I think the rule is it's got to be something sensational, something really strange and unusual."

"I see." The One-eyed Monkey became thoughtful.

"Well, but according to these people dragons are something strange and unusual, aren't they?" inquired Goldie. "I mean, if they think that we don't exist, then it would be strange and unusual if we did exist, wouldn't it?"

"Yes," said Opal. "Why don't you just put me in a bowl —"

"And me," Goldie interrupted.

"And Goldie," Opal carried on, "and show us to these people? 'Look, here are dragons,' you could say. And then that would be unusual, and they would put us on television, and then we could explain to everyone how they are poisoning the rivers and oceans."

"It could be dangerous," Rohit murmured.

"Why?"

"Well, they might think you were curiosities or fakes. They might want to lock you up and study you, or even dissect you and analyse you. And where would you be then?"

"I would be dead," replied Opal. "But without the river I'm in danger anyway. I want to take the risk. We must try to do something."

"And I'll go with Opal," Goldie put in. "After all, this is something that matters to everyone."

The others protested: they didn't want the two dragons risking their lives. Everyone was speaking at once when the One-eyed Monkey broke in. "I have an idea," she said, "that will minimise the risk and that will at the same time increase our chances of getting on television."

In a sentence or two she explained what she had in mind. The others began beaming. "Yes," Aditi said. "Yes. It is a good plan. Let's fill in the details. Perhaps we'll be able to make the six o'clock news. I think we're going to make a sensation."

The four adventurers, the two dragons and Roshan and Rohit settled down to plan the sensation. Roshan, Rohit and the Ant were sent off to watch the television studio and find out what they could. They were to report back in an hour. Opal, Aditi and Goldie sat down with a piece of paper and tried to work out exactly what they would say once they managed to get on television. And the Elephant, after she had reduced herself in size again, stationed herself in front of a puddle and began to practise squirting water. As for the One-eyed Monkey, she held her head between her hands and did her best to imagine absolutely everything that could possibly happen.

9

Being Heard

That afternoon they all made their way to the bus stop
again. Roshan and Rohit had reported on the location and
layout of the television studios and the Ant had even
drawn a map. The two dragons were curled up in a
goldfish bowl which Rohit was carrying. The Elephant
was nestling in Roshan's pocket. The One-eyed Monkey
was perched on Aditi's shoulder, but this time she was
wearing the cloak of invisibility, and was holding on tight
to a large flask. The Ant's matchbox with the magic clay
was safely inside Aditi's pocket. The Ant himself was
peering over the edge of the pocket. He would have liked
to have ridden with the One-eyed Monkey, but didn't
want to get too far from the clay. They were all feeling
tremendously excited and a little nervous about what was
likely to happen. "What if they won't let us in?" asked
the Elephant in a loud voice as they climbed onto the bus.

Roshan calmed her as best she could. "It's all right,
we have an alternative plan. But you must keep quiet.
People are beginning to stare."

"Why?" asked the Elephant.

"Well, if they saw me chatting away with an elephant in my pocket, they'd think it was strange."

"But that's good, isn't it?" insisted the Elephant. "After all, we want to be strange and unusual, don't we?"

Roshan smiled. "Yes," she said, "but not now. Do be quiet."

The Elephant subsided and did her best to be quiet until they reached the studios. Then she began jumping up and down with excitement, until Roshan had to put a hand over her to make her keep quiet.

"There's a Ms Jenkins who works here," Rohit whispered to Aditi. "She's a newscaster. Of the people who walked in and out this morning, she had the nicest face. Why don't we ask to see her?"

Everyone agreed. On the whole they all preferred to be straightforward and had decided to resort to tricks only if it became absolutely necessary. Accordingly, Aditi walked up to the doorkeeper and said politely, "We would like to see Ms Jenkins please."

The doorkeeper frowned at her. "Have you an appointment?"

"No," replied Aditi. "But we have a news item here in which we're sure she'd be interested."

The doorkeeper turned away and spoke into a telephone. They heard him say, "There's some children here. They say they have a news item."

He turned back to Aditi, "What is it? What is the news item?"

"Dragons," replied Aditi.

"Dragons," they heard the doorkeeper repeat into the receiver. They thought they heard someone laugh. Then the doorkeeper was glaring at them again.

"Wait here," he told them briefly. "She's coming down to see you."

It was obvious from his manner that he thought it was all a waste of time, but the children and the adventurers and the dragons waited quietly. In a few

minutes Ms Jenkins appeared. She smiled at the children. "Now," she said, "what's all this about dragons?"

"We've brought the dragons to show you," Aditi replied. "And we want to explain something to you so that you can then explain it to the rest of the world."

"You've brought dragons to show me?" Ms Jenkins sounded surprised. "Well, show them to me then."

Rohit showed her the goldfish bowl, which he had been covering up with his jacket, with the two dragons curled up inside.

Ms Jenkins stared at them. "They're beautiful," she murmured. "What are their names?"

"Opal and Goldie," Rohit replied. "Opal is a River Dragon and Goldie is a Sea Dragon."

"Yes. Well, they're charming. Thank you for showing them to me. I must go now." Ms Jenkins began to turn away. The children were aghast.

"But aren't dragons a news item? Aren't you going to put them on television? There's something we have to tell you," Roshan cried out.

Ms Jenkins turned back. She liked children. She smiled at Roshan. "But these aren't real dragons," she said. "These are some sort of exotic lizards. Real dragons would be a news item."

"But these are real dragons," Roshan protested. "What do you mean by 'unreal dragons'?"

Ms Jenkins laughed. "I suppose by 'real dragons' I mean 'unreal dragons' — the mythical creatures, the kind that don't exist."

Roshan began to play for time in the hope of giving the One-eyed Monkey or one of the others enough time to do something. "Please," she said, "please. If real dragons did exist, would you then say that they weren't dragons just because they did exist?"

Ms Jenkins laughed again. "Yes," she said. "I see your point. But these little ones aren't dragons. They're too tiny."

"But we've shrunk them!" Roshan was nearly crying with desperation. "They're much too big to be walking about the streets of London. They'd knock down buildings.

Even this square is barely large enough to hold one of them."

"That is a good explanation! But now I really must go." Ms Jenkins smiled in a friendly fashion and was about to turn away when suddenly her mouth fell open and she stood transfixed staring at something behind the children. A life-size dragon, who looked very much like Goldie, was taking up the entire square.

Aditi looked at the goldfish bowl which Rohit was still holding in his hands. Goldie was still curled up in it. It only took her a second or two to understand what had happened. She knew that the life-size dragon wouldn't last very long. She seized her chance. "Please," she said turning to Ms Jenkins, "now do you see that we really do know something about dragons? We have something important to tell you. Will you at least talk to us"

"Yes," Ms Jenkins muttered. "Yes, I'll talk to you, but first I must get a cameraman. That life-size dragon is big news." But even as she spoke the life-size dragon disappeared.

Ms Jenkins looked at the children. "You know something about all this, don't you? Come on. Come inside and give me some explanations."

They all crowded into Ms Jenkins' office. "Now," she demanded, "where did the big dragon come from?"

"The Ant made him," Aditi replied, "in order to show you what a life-size Goldie would look like."

"The Ant? I don't see any ant."

"No," Aditi said. "He's only little. He's in my pocket." She fetched him out of her pocket and set him on her shoulder.

Ms Jenkins peered at the Ant. "And is he also some mythical beast you've managed to shrink?" she inquired.

"No, no," Aditi answered. "That's his normal size."

"Well then," countered Ms Jenkins, "how do you expect me to believe your ridiculous story about being able to shrink creatures?"

"Well, there's me," they heard a small voice say. It seemed to be coming from Roshan's pocket. It was time, Roshan decided, to let the Elephant have her say. She took her out and put her down gently on the writing table in front of Ms Jenkins.

"Why are you so little?" asked Ms Jenkins feebly.

"Well, if I were my proper size, I would hardly be sitting on your writing table chatting with you now, would I?" replied the Elephant crossly. She was feeling a little bad-tempered from having been cooped up so long.

"No, no, I suppose you wouldn't be," murmured Ms Jenkins. "Tell me, are you able to return to your normal size?"

"Yes, of course," put in the One-eyed Monkey, who was getting impatient with how long it was taking to explain things. "We just wash off the ointment with a little water." She waved the flask she had been clutching in the air, having completely forgotten that she was wearing the cloak of invisibility.

Ms Jenkins stared in the direction of the voice. "Who was that?"

"That was the One-eyed Monkey," Aditi replied. "Do take off the cloak," she said to the One-eyed Monkey, "and make yourself visible."

The One-eyed Monkey took off the cloak and Ms Jenkins stared at her. "Did the Ant make you too?" she asked.

The One-eyed Monkey shook her head.

"But then why do you appear and disappear?"

The One-eyed Monkey explained about the cloak. Ms Jenkins nodded. She was trying to understand. "Are you your normal size?" she asked.

"Yes," said the One-eyed Monkey. "I am, but the Elephant isn't and the two dragons aren't."

"Can you make the Elephant bigger?"

"Yes," said the One-eyed Monkey. "That was what I was trying to explain to you. All we have to do is take off the ointment with a little water."

"Do it," commanded Ms Jenkins.

"Shall I?" asked the Elephant. "I'm supposed to squirt water on the dragons and myself if we're in any danger," she announced importantly.

But the One-eyed Monkey shook her head. "Your writing table would break," she told Ms Jenkins, "and we would have trouble getting the Elephant out of your office once she returned to her normal size. We'll try to explain everything if only you would please listen to us. Will you listen?"

"Yes," said Ms Jenkins and prepared to listen.

10

Making a Sensation

Ms Jenkins was a fair-minded woman. Having agreed to listen, she listened intelligently and attentively. The two dragons were taken out of the bowl and Opal was allowed to explain in detail what it was exactly that had happened to the river over the years. In the end Ms Jenkins was convinced that what they were saying really was true, but she did not want to make a fool of herself. "I'll need some proof that Opal and Goldie really are dragons," she told them. "Can't you give me a little demonstration?"

"No, not here," she added hastily. "I understand that if you were to return to your normal size here, you would break down the building. But you see, just to tell people that the river is being polluted hardly comes across as a news item."

The One-eyed Monkey nodded. "We understand the problem. Roshan and Rohit explained it to us. We need to create a sensation. We thought that the dragons in themselves would be sensational."

"Perhaps you're right," Ms Jenkins hesitated and then

made up her mind. "It's almost time for the six o' clock news. Come into the studio with me. I'll try to fit in an interview with you. But I'll have to get permission from my supervisor first."

They filed into the studio with Ms Jenkins and sat down quietly where she told them to, while she went off to consult her supervisor. All about them there were lights and cameras and cables trailing along the ground. No one paid any attention to them. At about one minute to six they saw Ms Jenkins returning. With her there was a tall man who was glaring at them and expostulating with her.

"How can you believe such silly stories?" he was saying to her in a superior fashion. "You'll turn our network into a laughing stock. Those are just lizards of some sort. Look, I'll show you." And with that he snatched the flask of water from the One-eyed Monkey and poured it into the goldfish bowl. For a second nothing happened and then under everyone's eyes the two dragons began to grow. The television crew trained their cameras on the dragons automatically. Aditi and the One-eyed Monkey were shouting to everyone to take cover. But people were transfixed. The bowl cracked and still the dragons

continued to grow. The Elephant scooped up the remaining
water and began to spray it over herself. She too began to
grow, but in the commotion no one noticed her. By now
Goldie and Opal were bumping the ceiling and the ceiling
had begun to fall on them.

"Take shelter under the dragons," the Elephant shouted, but the debris was falling fast, and she was kept busy rescuing people trapped under the bricks and mortar. Meanwhile the television cameras kept grinding on and broadcast all this on the six o'clock news. Opal and Goldie tried to keep still in order to minimise the damage, but once the entire studio had collapsed, they thought it might be wiser to remove themselves. The television cameras now pointed upwards and took pictures of the flying dragons.

As soon as she could, Ms Jenkins explained to her viewers what had happened. "We will keep you abreast with events," she promised them, "and will have an interview with Opal and Goldie as soon as possible."

Everyone began to try and clear the rubble. The supervisor, who had been knocked down by some flying plaster, came to his senses. "What happened?" he asked.

The One-eyed Monkey, who had been tending to him, looked at him thoughtfully. "I think," she said, "you created a sensation."

In the week that followed there was a great deal of work for Roshan and Rohit and the four adventurers and the two dragons. There were television appearances, newspaper articles and radio interviews. The two dragons were big news and the dragons and their friends made the most of their opportunity. In the end everyone had understood that dragons existed, that the rivers and the

oceans of the world were being poisoned and that the
Thames River Dragon was in particular danger unless
something was done soon. The cleaning up work was
begun, and though the task would take a long time, people
had at last become aware of the seriousness of the matter.

It was time for the four adventurers to say goodbye.
They were sorry to leave Roshan and Roshit. They said
goodbye over and over. Would the two children come
and visit them? Yes, Roshan and Rohit had said, yes, they
would. The Elephant was still sniffling a little. She had
grown particularly fond of Roshan and didn't want to
leave her. Roshan was doing her best to comfort her.
It was late in the evening and they were saying a last
farewell in Shadwell Park. The two dragons were standing
by to fly them home.

"But you can't stay with Aditi forever and ever," Rohit

said to Opal anxiously. "You yourself said that you need the river. What will you do when you return?"

"By then the upper reaches of the river will be clean again," Opal reassured him. "I'll live there."

"When will you return to London?" Roshan and Rohit asked simultaneously.

"When I am able," she told them gently. Then Aditi and the One-eyed Monkey and the Ant and the Elephant climbed aboard, and the dragons took off.

"Goodbye Goldie, goodbye Opal. See you again soon," Roshan and Rohit shouted and waved from Shadwell Park. And they did see each other again soon; but it was not until many years later, when Roshan and Rohit had left school and were grown-up young persons, that London again had her River Dragon.

For

Atibun, Ahad, Varun, Salma, Salma, Joseph,
Ayesha, Terry, Sharif, Rafia and Mukta

Class 12, Blue Gate Fields Junior School,
Tower Hamlets, London
1988

It's many later now, and the children must have grown up and
left the school some time ago, but perhaps they'll come across
this book somewhere and still enjoy the story and remember
how they had asked me to bring Aditi and her friends to England
all those years ago. — *Suniti Namjoshi*

Aditi and the Thames Dragon

ISBN 978-81-86895-57-3
© *text* Suniti Namjoshi
© *illustrations* Tulika Publishers
First published in India, 2002
Reprinted in 2005, 2007, 2018

Cover design by Roshini Pochont

Published by
Tulika Publishers, 305 Manickam Avenue, TTK Road, Alwarpet,
Chennai 600 018, India
email reachus@tulikabooks.com *website* www.tulikabooks.com

Printed and bound by
Sudarsan Graphics, Chennai, India

31901068456385